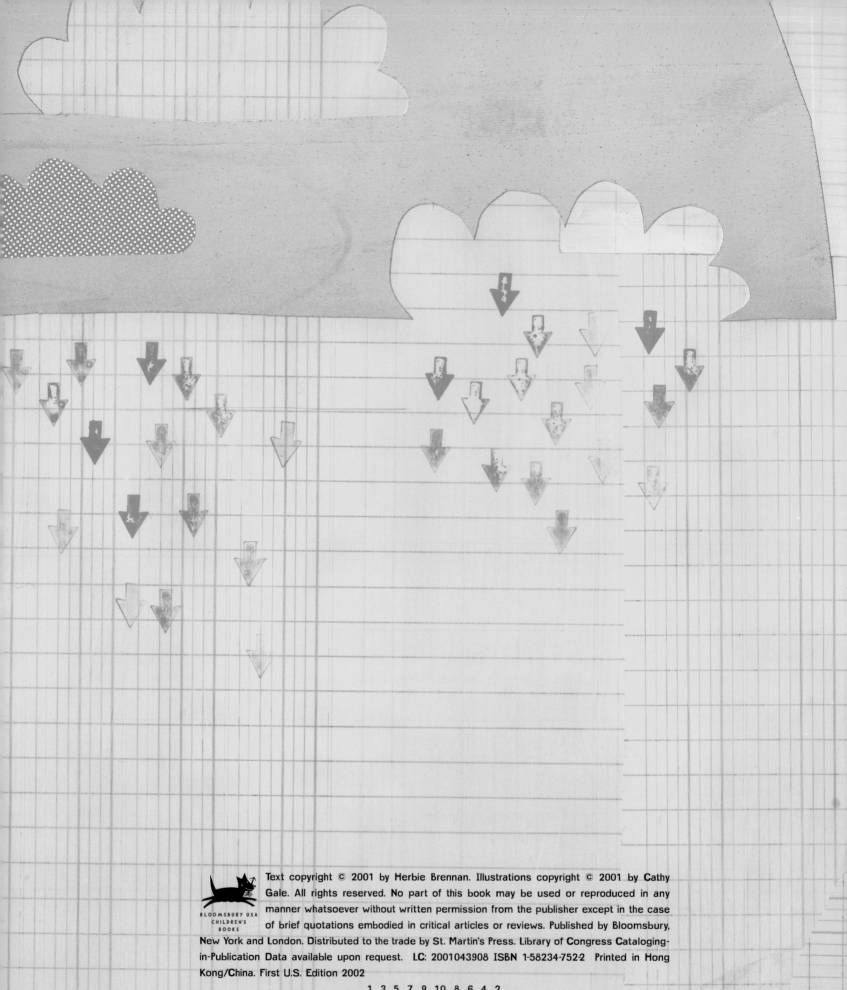

1 3 5 7 9 10 8 6 4 2

Bloomsbury Children's Books USA

175 Fifth Avenue   New York, NY 10010

FRANKENSTELLA
and the
VIDEO STORE MONSTER

By
Herbie Brennan
Illustrated by
Cathy Gale

Bloomsbury USA Children's Books
New York

There was a monster in the video store. It lurked in the dark corner where they kept the dusty old movies nobody wanted to rent anymore.
Although it crouched a lot and seemed quite small, it was actually

very, very big.

Anytime it got the chance, it ate customers.

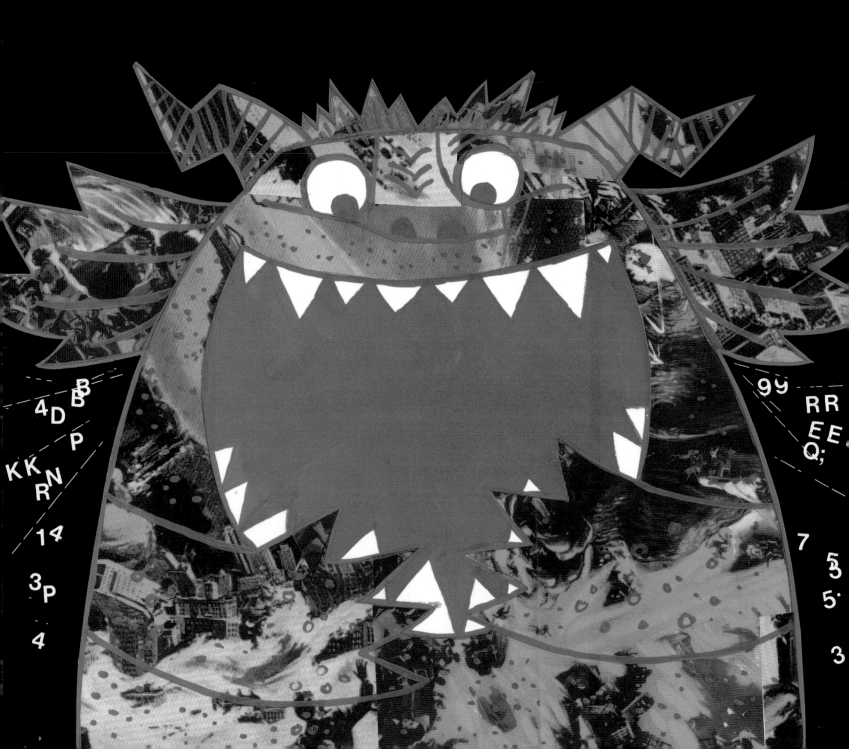

"Let's get a movie for tonight!" cried Stella's mother on the sidewalk just outside. "There's nothing but the World Cup on TV."

"Be careful of the video store monster," Stella said. Stella could sense monsters at a hundred yards.
"Oh, Stella, you have such a strange imagination!" trilled her mother, leaping through the door into the shop.

Stella followed cautiously. "See?" she asked.
Her mother laughed like tinkling bells.
"No monster here. No monster there. No
monster anywhere!" Stella's mother cried.

"No monster here," the video store man agreed.
He smiled and licked his teeth, which glistened wetly.
"It's over there," said Stella. "In that corner."

Stella's mother bounded straight into the corner.
"No monster here," she sang. "No monster there. No
monster anywh—"

At which point the monster ate her.

"Gets them every time," the video man chuckled.
He looked at Stella, and said, "Better watch out it
doesn't get you next."

But Stella wasn't listening.

She was too angry to listen.

She was as angry as a hornet, angry as a wasp.

She was as angry as a bull wearing rose-colored glasses.

She was so angry she began to change.

Her eyes turned red, her nose went flat. Long,
curling horns grew from her forehead.
Her teeth became enormous fangs.

She grew and grew until her head was
up against the ceiling, then grew some more
until she poked right through the roof.

Her muscles bulged so fiercely
that she knocked bricks from the walls.
Her feet grew very large and flat.

The video store monster tucked its tail between its legs and ran. Frankenstella chased the monster out of the video store.

Once it hit the open air, the monster grew larger than a double-decker bus, then larger than a house, then larger than an office block.

But Frankenstella grew larger still. She grew larger than a skyscraper. She grew larger than sixteen skyscrapers put together. She clumped after the video store monster on her huge flat skyscraper feet.

Frankenstella chased the monster down the river
and through the city.

Everybody cheered her on.

If her mother hadn't just been eaten, it would have been great fun.

"Help!" screamed the video store monster as Frankenstella caught up and thumped it on the back.

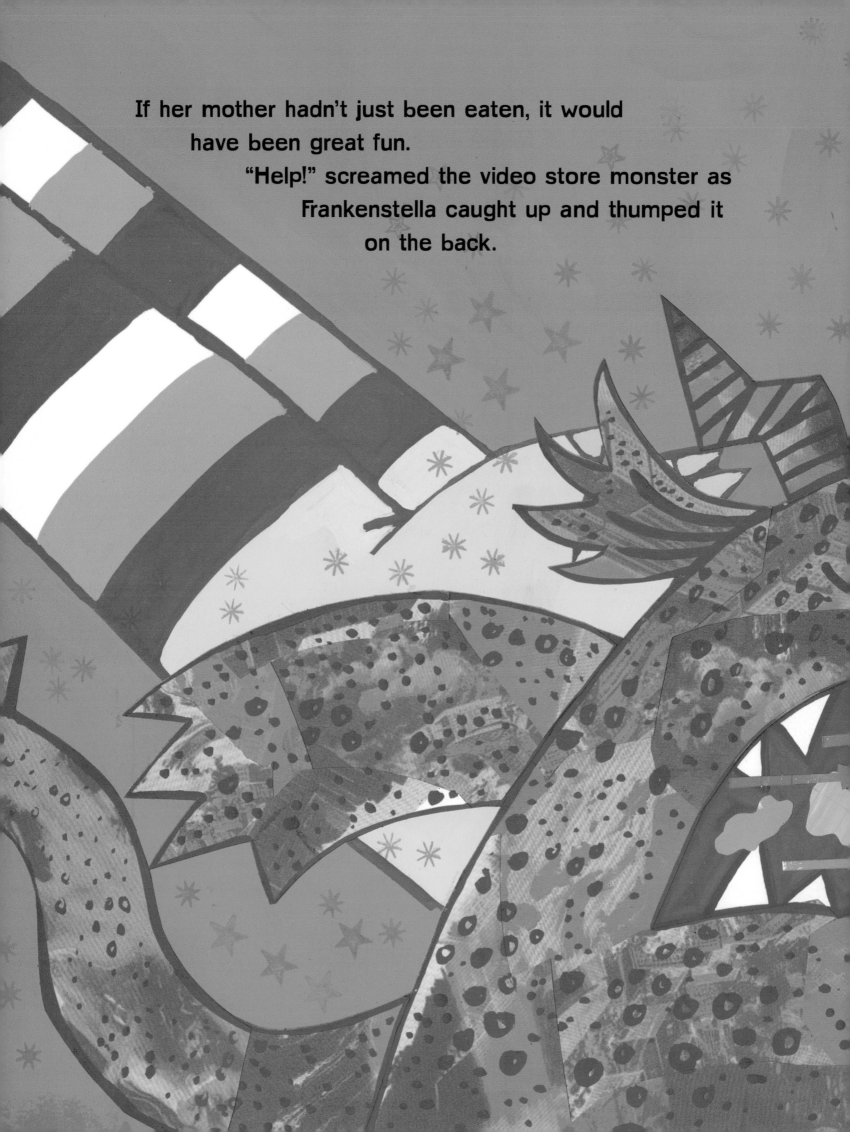

The video store monster burped rudely.
Stella's mother flew out of its mouth.
She was covered in green slime and confusion.

Frankenstella grabbed the
video store monster and hurled it
far out to sea where it couldn't eat people anymore.
(Any sailors it might meet would be far too salty.)

She took a breath to calm herself, and immediately she shrank back to her normal size, starting with her feet.

Her fangs became teeth. Her eyes became blue.

Her nose unsquashed itself.

Her muscles stopped bulging.

Her horns disappeared.

She had turned back
into Stella.

Her mother wiped the green slime from her eyes
and looked around.
"You see," she said. "No monster here. No monster there.
No monster anywhere."

She stood and reached out to take Stella's hand.
"In fact," she said, "there are no such things as monsters.
They're just in your strange imagination."
"Yes mother," Stella said politely.
But she smiled a secret smile.